LONGING FOR CHRISTMAS

25 Promises Fulfilled in Jesus

Advent Devotional for Teenagers

Edited by Chelsea Kingston Erickson,
Rooted Ministry

New
Growth
Press
newgrowthpress.com

New Growth Press, Greensboro, NC 27401
newgrowthpress.com
Copyright © 2024 by Rooted Ministry

Cover Design: Blake Cale, www.blake-cale.com
Interior Typesetting and eBook: Lisa Parnell, lparnellbookservices.com

ISBN: 978-1-64507-470-0 (Print)
ISBN: 978-1-64507-471-7 (eBook)

Library of Congress Cataloging-in-Publication Data on file

Printed in the United States of America

31 30 29 28 27 26 25 24   1 2 3 4 5

Contents

Introduction

Chelsea Kingston Erickson

Do you remember what it felt like to be a little kid at Christmastime?

I used to stay up late *weeks* before Christmas Eve, plotting my wish list by flashlight, long after lights out. Oh, I knew Christmas was about Jesus—but sadly that's not what kept me awake. I'd make myself nearly sick with longing, imagining fun with my cousins and the gifts to come under the tree.

Maybe your childhood excitement about Christmas was for a special LEGO set, a PlayStation, or an American Girl Doll. Perhaps you eagerly awaited a special family tradition or a celebration at church.

There's nothing quite like the anticipation of Christmas morning when we're young.

And then we grow up a bit. As we leave childhood behind, our experience of Christmas changes, especially as we encounter more of the world's suffering. Maybe you've lost a loved one to cancer, or your parents have divorced. Perhaps you feel lonely or anxious or angry. Maybe your friends have disappointed you or you're drowning in others' expectations for your performance in school or sports.

As a teenager, I often wished I could get back the thrill I used to feel at Christmastime. Instead, the holiday sometimes made me feel a little sad as I awoke to the real world with all its problems. Christmas never quite lived up to the hype I recalled from childhood. I'm guessing you have felt this too.

Longing for Something More

The loss we feel over our childhood wonder at Christmastime points to a deeper longing within all of us.

Author C. S. Lewis often wrote about the sense of bittersweet we all feel as we live in this world. He wrote that within each of us is an "inconsolable longing," or the feeling of missing something we can't quite name. When we long for the innocence of childhood or even for Christmases past, what we're really missing, Lewis said, is the life we were made for: life together with God, forever.

This desire human beings have to be with God is well documented in the pages of Scripture. In fact, the whole Bible is the story of how God creates a good world and puts people in it so that he may dwell with them. It's the story of how God makes a plan to rescue them even when his people reject him and go their own way.

Throughout the Old Testament, God makes promises to the very people who were running from him that he would send a rescuer, a Messiah, to save them. For centuries, God's people longed for the fulfillment of these promises.

Waiting for God's Promises

In the church calendar, we lean into longing during the season of Advent, which means *coming* or *arrival*. During Advent, we remember how God's people waited for a Savior, and how God promised to send his Son. During Advent, we remember how Jesus came long ago to a stable in Bethlehem, and how he will come again to fulfill every last promise God has ever made.

Over the next twenty-five days, we'll look at some of these promises and how they help us to prepare our hearts for Christmas morning. Each day you'll read about a specific promise God made—and how he has fulfilled each one in Jesus Christ. It's important to note that we've ordered the promises chronologically through history, not in the order our Bibles record them. This is to help you get a sense of the time line of biblical history. As we journey through the Old Testament, I hope you'll see how its story causes us to eagerly wait for the Savior.

The authors of each chapter have been where you are. They know what it is like to feel lonely and left out, worn down and weary of this world. But each of them has found hope in the good news of Jesus's life, death, and resurrection. It's a hope we want to share with you.

If you feel a little melancholy or downright disappointed this Christmas season, take heart. All of the longing we feel—for a better world, for renewed innocence, for things to be made right—will finally be met in Jesus. As we lean into longing together, I hope you'll experience something of the childlike anticipation for Christmas morning—not for gifts that await you under the tree, but for God's promised gift of his Son.

The best Christmas mornings of our childhoods are only a small taste of the good and beautiful world to come when Jesus returns to make all things right.

Day 1

Longing for What Has Been Lost

Chris Li

"I will put enmity between you and the woman,
and between your offspring and her offspring;
he shall bruise your head,
and you shall bruise his heel." (Genesis 3:15)

Have you ever had a blue Christmas?

My family's Christmases growing up included cousins, aunts, uncles, and grandparents at our home for a loud and happy meal. But after my grandpa died, I remember going on a late-night walk with my mom and reminiscing about what Christmas used to be for our family. That first year especially, Christmas felt sad.

Unfortunately for many, Christmas can be a painful, stressful, and lonely time. From disappointment in our relationships with family and friends to reminders of sickness and death, the holidays can subtly highlight the brokenness of our world and the darkness in our lives. But God's Word reminds us that we can take comfort and find hope in a Savior—a Savior God promised us from the very beginning.

All the pain we experience can be traced back to the Garden of Eden, where the first human beings rejected God's rule. The Bible calls this sin, and we experience the traces of it everywhere. Friends leave us out or leave us behind, parents fight or get divorced, and we hurt others with our actions and words too.

Sin is choosing to live life on our own terms. Our sin separates us from who we are meant to be, from other people, and worst of all, from God. As we battle with sin, we need someone to help us be victorious because—in case you haven't noticed—we cannot save ourselves. This need we have for a rescuer is what Christmas is all about.

THE GOD WHO MAKES PROMISES

At the beginning of human history, God made a garden and placed the first two people, Adam and Eve, within it. What they had with God was special—a close relationship. They would go for walks with God, joyfully work to cultivate the land, and eat from the bounty God had given them. But God told them there was one tree from which they could not eat.

Adam and Eve listened to an impostor, a serpent who deceived them. They rebelled against God and ate of the tree of the knowledge of good and evil. When they did, sin entered the world.

Immediately after darkness broke into the world, God made a promise to one day overcome it. God spoke to the serpent: "He shall bruise your head, and you shall bruise his heel." This strange promise was the whisper of a Savior to come. God promised that one day, he would restore his close relationship with his people and bring them back to paradise.

THE GOD WHO KEEPS PROMISES

When Jesus came into the world, he fulfilled God's long-awaited promise. As we trace the offspring of Adam and Eve throughout the Bible, we see that their family tree leads to Jesus, the Messiah.

From the offspring of Adam and Eve, Jesus came to crush sin and Satan. But how? Jesus was bruised on the cross for our sin. As Jesus laid down his life, Satan was also bruised as his scheme to end God's plan of salvation failed. When Jesus nailed our sin to the cross and rose from the dead, he delivered the fatal blow (Colossians 2:13–15).

Christmas can be a difficult time, especially if you are dealing with the heartache of sin and darkness, both in others and in yourself. When you spend time with friends and family, it can feel like things will never get better. When you reflect on the year, you may feel lost, like a failure, burned out, or drifting away from God.

Christmas is not about God telling us to toughen up, try harder, or be better. Instead, Christmas calls us to remember that God himself came down to earth to do what we could not do for ourselves. God saw our sin and the sin of the world. He sent Jesus to fulfill his promise from so long ago. One day, Jesus will come again to restore the paradise he created in the garden.

God is faithful to his Word, and he wants a relationship with you! No matter what you are going through this Christmas, look to him as the one who is able to rescue and save.

Questions for Further Reflection

1. What areas of brokenness are highlighted for you this holiday season?
2. What parts of your life seem beyond rescue?
3. There is nothing so dark that Jesus cannot (and has not) already overcome. In what ways does this truth offer you a sense of rest? How does the fact that Jesus overcomes all help you rejoice?

Closing Prayer

Father, we thank you for Jesus—that from the beginning you knew we needed a Savior to rescue us from our sin. Even though there is darkness and despair around us, you are present and faithful, giving us hope. In both our pain and our sin, our victory is in Christ who has crushed our Enemy, Satan. Spirit, help us to remember Jesus during this season and to rejoice in what he has done for us.

Day 2

Longing for Peace

Chelsea Kingston Erickson

Now the LORD said to Abram, "Go from your country and your kindred and your father's house to the land that I will show you. And I will make of you a great nation, and I will bless you and make your name great, so that you will be a blessing. I will bless those who bless you, and him who dishonors you I will curse, and in you all the families of the earth shall be blessed."
(Genesis 12:1–3)

Have you ever thought about how much hostility exists between groups of people and nations in our world? As we look to history and even to our present day, it's so apparent that human beings are prone to dividing against one another: *Slavery. The Holocaust. Apartheid. Genocide in Rwanda. Racism. The war on Ukraine. Conflict in the Middle East.*

We regularly see groups of people pushed to the sidelines because they look or act or live somewhere different. Nearly every day we hear stories of these divisions in the news. Maybe you have even experienced the painful reality of prejudice yourself as you live in our sin-torn world.

The sin we read about in Genesis 3 extends not only to individual relationships, but to groups of people and whole nations. If you've ever felt sadness, frustration, or even rage over these broken human relationships, the story of the Bible comes as really good news. From the beginning God has been working out a plan to rescue people from every corner of the world, to bless them and include them in his family.

THE GOD WHO MAKES PROMISES

In Genesis 12:1–3, we read about God's promises to a man called Abram (later renamed Abraham). There was nothing special about Abram; in fact, he and his father were idol-worshippers (Joshua 24:2) who had no knowledge of the one true God. And yet *God* initiated a relationship with Abram, including Abram in his plan to rescue the world.

Later in Genesis, God explains his blessing will come through Abraham's offspring, picking up on the promise to Eve in the Garden from yesterday's reading (Genesis 18:18; 22:18; 26:4; 28:14). At the time Abraham and his wife Sarai are old and childless, so it seems impossible that God could actually fulfill his word to them.

God does all he promised for Abraham, giving him a son, Isaac, whose descendants become the nation of Israel. And throughout the Old Testament, God often includes other nations—even Israel's enemies—in the blessings he has promised.[1] Still, the nations war against one another and human sin continues.

THE GOD WHO KEEPS PROMISES

All of God's blessings to Abraham find their ultimate fulfillment when Jesus arrives on the scene. He is the offspring from Abraham's line who "comes to make God's blessings flow," as we sing at Christmas.

Jesus regularly engaged with people across ethnicities and backgrounds, inviting them to trust him in faith. He lived, died, and rose again in their place and ours. When we come

---

1. Here are some other Scriptures in which we see God including the nations: Exodus 3:16–22; 9:20–21; 12:38; 18; Joshua 2; Ruth 1:1–5; 4:13–17; Jonah 3:6–10.

into a relationship with Jesus, he welcomes us into this diverse family God promised so long ago.

The New Testament shows how the early Church embraced God's mission to include the nations of the world. What started as a Jewish movement quickly expanded to include the Gentiles (or non-Jews), including men, women, and children from all walks of life. Today, Christianity is the most socially and ethnically diverse movement in the world.

In Revelation, the final book of the Bible, we read that when Jesus returns, "a great multitude that no one could count, from every nation, tribe, people and language" will gather at God's throne to worship him (Revelation 7:9 NIV). This beautifully multiethnic gathering results not from human effort, but from God's saving work in Jesus.

From the beginning, God has been pursuing people who might otherwise be at odds with one another, inviting us into relationship. Like Abraham, we do nothing to deserve God's blessing; we receive it through grace alone. Also like Abraham, God blesses us so that we might bless others in his name, bringing the good news about Jesus to people from all cultures and backgrounds.

QUESTIONS FOR REFLECTION

1. What conflict in our world today causes you to feel sadness or anger? Bring these feelings to God in prayer, knowing he cares for the nations of the world.

2. What are some of the messages we hear about the solution to broken human relationships? How do these compare to the gospel, which says we can't save ourselves but need Jesus to rescue us?

3. How could it help you to remember the way God has included you in Christ? When do you most need to remember his good plans for our world?

CLOSING PRAYER

Lord, I experience the effects of sin in my relationships, and I see it in the way people everywhere struggle to get along. Thank you for sending Jesus to rescue me. Help me to remember the good news that you are pursuing people from every nation and tribe. Please make me brave to point others to you. Amen.

Day 3

Longing for Redemption

Anna Meade Harris

"For I know that my Redeemer lives,
and at the last he will stand upon the earth." (Job 19:25)

Imagine this: In the span of one week your GPA tanks, Coach benches you without warning, your girlfriend dumps you, your little brother wrecks your car, and your parents ground you. To top it off, your best friend (the one person who is still talking to you) assures you that all these troubles are your own fault.

That would qualify as a bad week.

All of us have had times where it feels like everything is falling apart, but few have had the troubles of a godly man named Job.

THE GOD WHO MAKES PROMISES

In one day, Job's entire fortune in livestock is destroyed and he hears that his ten children have been killed in a tornado. Finding him covered from head to toe with painful sores, Job's wife urges him to "curse God and die" (Job 2:9). His best friends come to comfort him, but they soon tire of watching him pick at his scabs. They tell Job his misery is the result of his own sin.

Eventually, the poor man gets fed up. Feeling accused by his friends, his servants, his wife, and even God (Job 10:6–22),

Job explodes . . . with a remarkable prophecy of hope against all evidence to the contrary.

Even in his suffering, Job declares that he already has the Redeemer he needs. While we may know the word *redeemer* only from church buildings and old hymns, the term had a very specific meaning in the Ancient Near East. *Redeemer* was "the name given to the next of kin whose duty it was to redeem, ransom, or avenge one who had fallen into debt or bondage."[2] In one loaded word, we understand that the *Redeemer* God promised to send will not only pay our debt and rescue us from bondage, he will claim us as family.

THE GOD WHO KEEPS PROMISES

This long-awaited Redeemer—Jesus—will declare that Job is not to blame for all his misfortunes. Even more glorious, on the cross Jesus will pay the price for the sins that Job *did* commit, freeing him from the bondage of sin and death. Whether we are the victims of someone else's sin (the unjust accusations of Job's friends), or of living in a fallen world (the tornado that killed his children), or if we are held in bondage to our own sin (that's all of us, according to Romans 3:23), Jesus claims to be our closest relative, the One who redeems us from it all.

What's more, thousands of years before Jesus was born into a human body, Job uses the present tense verb to describe him. Jesus was alive when all of the bad things happened in your life. He lives even now to pray for you (Hebrews 7:25). Because he has overcome death, he will live with you eternally. Yesterday, today, and forever, your Redeemer is alive (Hebrews 13:8). Until he stands on earth again, he is working for your redemption.

---

2. Stanley Leathes, "Job," in *Ellicot's Commentary for English Readers*, ed. Charles John Ellicot (London: Cassell and Company, 1905) via *Bible Hub*, s.v. "Job 19:25," accessed March 4, 2023, https://biblehub.com/commentaries/job/19-25.htm.

So, when you are having your terrible, horrible, no good, very bad day (or week or year), when everything goes wrong and you feel completely alone, know that *your Redeemer lives.* Through his life, death, and resurrection, Jesus defeated death and sin and every kind of suffering.

The troubles of this life are painful but temporary; Jesus is permanent. He is with you now and forever. On that day when your faith becomes sight, you will be close enough to see the smile you bring to his face.

QUESTIONS FOR REFLECTION

1. Where do you turn when it seems that everything is falling apart? Netflix? Gaming? Food, alcohol, or porn? Job teaches us to lament (pour out painful feelings to God in prayer) and to declare what we know to be true about Jesus. Read the Psalms, like 22, 27, 31, 42, 55, 86. You'll find Jesus in every one.

2. Think about a time when you *have* brought a heap of troubles on yourself. Do you know that you can run to God even when you have really screwed up? That he is not surprised by your failures or angry with you? We need Jesus to redeem us because we cannot redeem ourselves. See Psalm 51.

3. Revelation 22:4 echoes this prophecy from Job, saying that when Jesus returns, those who believe in him "will see his face." How does it make a difference in your hardships to know that you will one day see God for yourself?

CLOSING PRAYER

Father, sometimes I feel crushed by the weight of things gone wrong and abandoned by people I thought would help me. But your Word says that you are the lifter of my head (Psalm 3:3). Give me eyes of faith, I pray, and raise my eyes to see you, Jesus, my Redeemer who lives.

Day 4

Longing for Forever

Kendal Conner

"When your days are fulfilled and you lie down with your fathers,
I will raise up your offspring after you, who shall come from your
body, and I will establish his kingdom. He shall build a house
for my name, and I will establish the throne of his kingdom
forever. I will be to him a father, and he shall be to me a son."
(2 Samuel 7:12–14a)

The idea of forever can often feel magical, such as when we
have a good day and we wish it could last forever. Or when
we eat something delicious and we wish we could eat only
that food forever. At other times, forever can also feel more
daunting than delightful. A difficult school year might feel
like it will last forever, or we may face a family situation that
seems never to end. In times like those, our hope is often in
the truth that it won't last forever.

This is why it can be hard for us to imagine the full goodness of what God means when he promises a King who will
reign forever and a kingdom that will never end. However,
for God's people, the promise of a forever kingdom is exactly
what makes this moment in the story of God's salvation so
significant.

THE GOD WHO MAKES PROMISES

God's promise to King David in 2 Samuel 7 was a turning
point in the story of God's people. For the first time, God

revealed that not only would the savior of the world be the son of man, he would also be the Son of God and the King of Israel.

Let's stop to consider the circumstances of this promise. God had just helped David defeat his enemies and, as a sign of worship, David wants to build a house for God. Yet God reverses the script. First God forbids David to build him a house, and then in an act of unprecedented grace, God promises to build *David's* house. In this house, established by God himself, David's offspring would reign *forever*. In the ancient world, kings and kingdoms were always vulnerable to conquer at the hands of their enemies. So this promise of an enduring kingdom would have been stunning in its comfort.

This is the word I want us to hold onto today—*forever*. The promise of forever that God gave to David was not crushing, but comforting. This forever kingdom would be nothing like his current one. It would be perfect.

THE GOD WHO KEEPS PROMISES

While many of David's descendants sat on the throne after him, each one ultimately experienced an end to his reign. That is, until the One who came who was not only the Son of David, but also the Son of God. God's promise to David about this eternal King would be perfectly and completely met in the birth of one child. It was this promise to David that made the advent news announced to Mary at the beginning of Luke so meaningful.

"And the Lord God will give him the throne of his father David, and he will reign over the house of Jacob forever, and of his kingdom there will be no end" (Luke 1:32b–33).

Because Jesus was both God and man, he did what no other king ever could. He faced the greatest enemy of any kingdom—death—and defeated it. In his resurrection, Jesus established a kingdom that nothing can ever destroy. It is a kingdom that will last forever.

Now, in another act of unprecedented grace, Jesus extends this kingdom to us. And he does not ask us to build anything for him in return. He does not consider our grades, performance, or popularity for entrance into this kingdom. Instead, by grace alone, he brings us into a kingdom that is unshakable and eternal. He gives us a new identity as children of God, sons and daughters that will one day reign with him *forever*.

QUESTIONS FOR FURTHER REFLECTION

1. Why did it matter that the Savior of the world would be both God and human?
2. Can you imagine what our forever home with God might look like? What comfort does a forever kingdom bring to those who follow Jesus?
3. If Christ's kingdom is forever, how does that change the way we live now?

CLOSING PRAYER

Lord, we thank you that you are always faithful to your promises. We pray that when all around us seems to fail, you would remind us that your kingdom never will. Help us to keep our eyes always on the hope of our forever home with you.

Longing for Comfort

Mark Howard

> A company of evildoers encircles me;
> they have pierced my hands and feet—
> I can count all my bones—
> they stare and gloat over me;
> they divide my garments among them,
> and for my clothing they cast lots. (Psalm 22:16b–18)

"Seriously, God—what gives?"

If you haven't said this yet in your life—spoiler alert—you will. Merry Christmas! ‾_(ツ)_/‾

Because let's be real—the holidays can be awful, making everything feel more intense. Our parents' divorces, fights with friends, breakups, deaths, all we don't like about ourselves and our lives can sting a bit deeper with the "glad tidings of great joy" swirling around us.

The pressure to keep it all together, to *look* "merry and bright" can be overwhelming. But you don't need to pretend that everything is okay. Every moment doesn't have to be Instagram-worthy.

THE GOD WHO MAKES PROMISES

King David, the author of Psalm 22, was no stranger to suffering. He was a man after God's own heart, and yet he wrote a song that started with, "My God, my God, why have you forsaken me?" (Psalm 22:1). He had a deep and intimate relationship with God, yet David continued, "O my God, I cry by day, but you do not answer, and by night, but I find no rest," (Psalm 22:2).

What we hear in Psalm 22 is raw lament to God, as David spills his sorrow, grief, and feelings of abandonment before the Lord. The fact that this psalm was recorded and included in Scripture provides a promise to us that God can handle even our deepest groanings and our most raw questions.

And what's even more amazing to me is that we know from Scripture that God *heard* him. More than that, in this psalm we learn that God promises to make our grief his own. King David's words point to a greater King to come who would take all our suffering upon himself.

THE GOD WHO KEEPS PROMISES

Over a millennium after David wrote Psalm 22, Jesus chooses this very psalm to be among his last words (Matthew 27:46). Reread the verses at the start of this chapter and see how closely they speak to Jesus's crucifixion. Jesus is encircled by robbers, Roman soldiers, and Pharisees scoffing at his death. His hands and feet are pierced as he's nailed to the cross. His garments are divided with the casting of lots by soldiers who know he is doomed to die.

But unlike King David, Jesus was not spared death.

If you're hurting this holiday season, remember that King Jesus also knows what it feels like to be miserable. "We do not have a high priest who is unable to sympathize with our weaknesses." (Hebrews 4:15). Jesus's love compelled him to endure death to deliver us. His resurrection gives us hope to press on. And Jesus's ascension to heaven means that he has sent his Spirit, our Comforter, to be with us until Jesus returns in victory.

So, feel free to lament before God—David did. Jesus did. It's okay for you to lament as well. God promises to listen and share in your suffering. Remember that God's Spirit is within you—let his comfort fill you.

And when Jesus returns, no longer will God feel distant. No longer will we cry, "Why?" in misery. Rather, "the dwelling place of God" will be among us, and God himself "will wipe away every tear" from our eyes, "and death shall be no more, neither shall there be mourning, nor crying, nor pain anymore, for the former things have passed away" (Revelation 21:3–4). This, too, is God's promise.

Questions for Further Reflection

1. What leaves you feeling broken and alone this holiday season?
2. Where and how can you embrace God's promise of the Holy Spirit to comfort you?
3. Who around you needs to be embraced with understanding in their suffering, rather than judgment?

Closing Prayer

Merciful God, take my misery, sadness, and disappointment as your own, and nail it to the cross. God of grace, give me your peace and fill me with your Spirit in such a way that I know in the depths of my being that you are with me and will never forsake me.

Longing for Rescue

Rebecca Lankford

I waited patiently for the LORD;
he inclined to me and heard my cry.
He drew me up from the pit of destruction,
out of the miry bog,
and set my feet on a rock,
making my steps secure. (Psalm 40:1–2)

If you've ever seen the 1987 movie *The Princess Bride*, you might remember the scene where the two protagonists, Wesley and Princess Buttercup, are trekking through a dangerous forest. In the forest, Buttercup falls into a pit of quicksand. She's sunk so deeply that viewers are left in suspense, wondering if the pit has swallowed her alive. Thankfully, Wesley acts quickly: he grabs hold of a vine, dives into the pit, and uses the vine to pull himself and Buttercup back up to safety. Had Wesley not gone into the pit himself, Buttercup would not have survived.

THE GOD WHO MAKES PROMISES

Psalm 40 tells us about a different kind of pit. We don't know the exact circumstances that led to David penning the words of Psalm 40. Perhaps he wrote this psalm in response to running from King Saul's attempted murder. Or maybe after a particularly intense military battle. Maybe David was in a pit of his own sin and shame (see Psalm 51).

Although we don't know the full story, it's clear that David knows a thing or two about needing to be rescued. More importantly, David knows that he can cry out to God, his true rescuer, for deliverance. David's words in Psalm 40 provide assurance that one day, the truest rescuer of all would come—not just for David, but for all who trust in God.

David begins this psalm by giving thanks for God's past rescue in his life. He remembers how God heard his cries, rescued him from his sin and suffering, set his feet upon a rock, and gave him a new song of praise (vv. 1–3).

Now, it seems, David is in the pit again. He is surrounded by evils "beyond number" (v. 12). Just like Buttercup, David is at the bottom of a pit and is in need of someone to rescue him. Because David remembers the ways in which God has rescued him in the past, he is confident that God will be his "help and deliverer" (v. 17).

We don't know how exactly God delivered David from this particular "miry bog." But we do know how God would ultimately answer his cries—and ours—for rescue.

THE GOD WHO KEEPS PROMISES

Christmas is the celebration of the greatest and most successful rescue mission of all time. In Jesus, God has rescued us from the deepest of pits: sin and death. He knew when it came to our salvation that we were as helpless as someone at the bottom of a pit of quicksand.

So, God put on flesh to save us. He trudged through the mud and sludge of our messy, sinful, broken world. Jesus bore the punishment for our sin and rose triumphantly over death. He picked us up, carried us to level ground, bringing us to new life.

Therefore, we have the assurance that he will deliver us from every "miry bog" we face. With David, we can recount all the times God has "made haste to help us" (v. 13).

You might be in a pit like David right now. Maybe you feel your feet slipping beneath you and fear that the miry bog will swallow you up. May God's words to you in Psalm 40 remind you of his sure and certain plan to rescue you. In this Advent season of waiting, may his Spirit accompany you and strengthen you to "wait patiently" for his deliverance (v. 1).

In Jesus, you have a capable and kind rescuer. Nothing can keep him from loving you (v. 11). He is so dedicated to rescuing you that he was willing to leave the glory of Heaven in order to bring you back to himself. No matter what miry bog you face, Jesus has rescued you. And he will rescue you again.

QUESTIONS FOR REFLECTION

1. In this psalm, David mentions that God has given him an "open ear" and that "the Lord takes thought of [him]" (vv. 6, 17). How does the fact that the Lord listens to you and takes thought of you impact the way you relate to him?

2. How can you, like David, speak of God's "faithfulness and salvation?" Can you think of specific people or places where you can share the work God has done in your life?

3. Are you in a particular "pit" right now? How does this psalm encourage you in the midst of that pit? It might be helpful to reflect on how God has drawn you out of previous "pits" in the past.

CLOSING PRAYER

Father, thank you for sending your Son Jesus to rescue us from the deepest pit. Thank you that we can cry out to you for rescue and trust you to deliver us. Help us to wait patiently and expectantly for your salvation. Amen.

Day 7

Longing for Acceptance

Connor Coskery

The stone that the builders rejected
has become the cornerstone.
This is the LORD's doing;
it is marvelous in our eyes. (Psalm 118:22–23)

Have you ever felt rejected? My sophomore year of high school, I was left off the roster for the state championship football game. I had worked hard all season but the coach decided to field an upperclassman in my place. I had given it my all, and still I hadn't made the cut. The feeling of rejection crushed me.

Maybe you haven't experienced rejection on the athletic field, but chances are you have felt the pain of rejection elsewhere. Whether it's restrictive parents, drama-filled friend groups, or a stingy college admissions department, life provides ample opportunity for rejection, especially as you get older. What can be surprising is rejection following success instead of failure. The most painful times are when we have performed well or tried our best, yet still feel like we aren't enough.

THE GOD WHO MAKES PROMISES

Psalm 118 contains a promise that God's love will hold you fast in times when you feel the weight of painful rejection.

The psalmist describes builders rejecting a very important part of the construction process—the cornerstone. In ancient times, the cornerstone was essential because it united the different aspects of a structure and held it together. Picture the outer piece of a Jenga tower. If you take that piece away, the whole tower falls apart.

The psalmist's image of the builders foreshadows something beyond bad construction practice. God was promising to send a Savior, but this promised rescuer would experience rejection from the people he came to save. And yet, the psalmist rejoices, saying "This is the LORD's doing," even calling the cornerstone's rejection "marvelous" (Psalm 118:23). As we read these words, they might strike us as odd. The psalmist is pointing to something wonderful that will come from the rejection of this promised rescuer.

THE GOD WHO KEEPS PROMISES

During his earthly ministry, Jesus would identify himself as the cornerstone of his Church (Matthew 21:42; Ephesians 2:19–22), the singular piece that would hold everything else together.

What's more, salvation came through the life, death, and resurrection of Jesus. It's resurrection that finally completed the psalmist's rejoicing. When the Enemy appeared victorious, the marvelous reality is that God raised Jesus and replaced sadness with joy, defeating sin and death. The Christmas season reminds us that God always keeps his promises.

Jesus provides rest for the weary and acceptance for the rejected. When you trust in him, you are no longer defined by whatever *no* you have received. Instead, God looks at you as you are in Jesus, not as you are in yourself. God looks at you and says, "You are my dear child; I am delighted with you."

The holiday season can be exhausting. For me, it always began with final exams, which led into Christmas parties and ended with a dose of family drama. Often, our expectations are disappointed. Maybe that friend doesn't show up to your party. Or your grades are lower than expected. Where exhaustion and misplaced expectations exist, *rejection* often lurks close by. Perhaps you can relate?

If so, hear the promise of the gospel held out in Psalm 118. The good news of Jesus is that the true cornerstone was rejected so that you would never be rejected. In Christ, God brings you near so that you can rejoice in his victory song. As the cornerstone, Jesus holds all things together.

The remedy for rejection is the gospel. You no longer have to hold it all together in order to be accepted. The pain of rejection is replaced with Christ's loving welcome.

The Christmas season reminds us to marvel at God's plan for salvation, which meant sending the Savior as a baby to live and die so that you could become a son or daughter of the King of Heaven. Because of Jesus, you are accepted, loved, and adopted into God's family. When you know Jesus as the cornerstone, you are secure and brought near. You don't have to have it all together, and you can rest in God's love, knowing that he will hold you fast.

QUESTIONS FOR REFLECTION

1. Have you ever felt rejected? How did it make you feel?
2. How does Jesus, the cornerstone who was rejected in your place, offer you rest?
3. Is there anything in your life that you need to hand over to Jesus?

CLOSING PRAYER

Father, thank you for the salvation you purchased for me in Jesus. Remind me, Holy Spirit, that even when

I feel alone, you are near. Help me to believe that I don't have to hold everything together because Jesus holds me fast.

Longing for New Life

Kendal Conner

> "In that day I will raise up
> the booth of David that is fallen
> and repair its breaches,
> and raise up its ruins
> and rebuild it as in the days of old,
> that they may possess the remnant of Edom
> and all the nations who are called by my name,"
> declares the LORD who does this. (Amos 9:11–12)

I love books. There is nothing quite like grabbing a warm blanket, a new book, and getting lost in a good story. Books offer an escape from reality because, in any good story, justice will prevail and love will win.

And isn't that ultimately what most of us want? Whether it's through video games, movies, or books, we long for the safety and certainty of a truly good story. Knowing a story will inevitably end well actually allows us to enjoy the story more—no matter the ride it takes us on to get there.

If we are honest, most of us long for a bit of predictability in the world as well. Maybe this is why we find joy in escaping into a movie, book, or video game every now and then. We all want to know, without a doubt, that good will prevail and all will be made right. The promise of predictability disarms us and offers hope no matter where the story takes us.

It is God who has created in us this longing for certainty. He gave us hearts that crave assurance, knowing that he alone is the one who can meet that desire.

THE GOD WHO MAKES PROMISES

Today's Scripture drops us into the story of God's people in a time of great uncertainty. The prophet Amos has traveled back to the "hometown" of his people—to a city in Israel called Bethel, which means the "house of God." It was here in this town that God had met with Abraham's grandson Jacob, reminding him of the promises God had made to his family.

When Amos writes hundreds of years later, the kingdom of Israel has been divided in two and the Israelites to the north seem to have forgotten their God. They are deep into worshipping idols. They have turned from seeking justice toward pursuing evil. In the same place God once spoke hope to Jacob, he now gives Amos a word of warning and ruin for Israel: because of Israel's unfaithfulness, God will allow the Assyrians to take God's people captive as exiles in the years to come. Hope seems lost.

But God's story never ends with ruin. God also gives Amos a promise of certain hope.

In Amos 9:11–12, God promises resurrection on the other side of the coming ruin. God will bring his people back from exile and reunite them as one, restoring what he promised to Jacob. He will resurrect the fallen kingdom of David—but this resurrection will come in the most unpredictable way.

THE GOD WHO KEEPS PROMISES

After several hundred years of ruin, a son is born to a man named Joseph, a descendant of David, a descendant of Jacob. Yet, this child is more than the son of man; he is the only begotten Son of God himself. Through this baby, God kept his promise to Israel. This child is the very offspring of

Abraham, Isaac, and Jacob—who would finally, and fully, bring blessing to all the nations.

Jesus—the son of man and Son of God—bore the weight of what sin had ruined through his death on the cross. Because of sin, all of us have fallen short of the glory of God (Romans 3:23). Yet, by his resurrection, God has made a way to raise what has fallen to all who would come to Jesus by faith (Ephesians 2:8–9).

In Jesus, God rebuilds his house at last; he irrevocably raises the tent of David. Only, this time, the kingdom is not a single nation, but a people from every nation, tribe, and tongue.

While we will experience moments of ruin, we do not have to despair. For all who come to Jesus by faith, the end of the story is certain. What once was ruined will be eternally raised.

QUESTIONS FOR FURTHER REFLECTION

1. Is it ever hard for you to trust that God's promises are certain?
2. God fulfilled his promise in Amos 9:11 in an unpredictable way. What might that tell us about how God works?
3. How can knowing the end of the story of the Bible give you comfort when you experience moments of ruin?

CLOSING PRAYER

God, thank you for building us a certain and eternal home in your Son, Jesus. Make us a people of hope as we take comfort in your promises. By your Holy Spirit, give us eyes to see what you have rebuilt, and are rebuilding, in our own lives. Help us to faithfully labor alongside you as we seek to be a blessing to those around us. Amen.

Day 9

Longing to Be Enough

Rebecca Heck

But you, O Bethlehem Ephrathah,
who are too little to be among the clans of Judah,
from you shall come forth for me
one who is to be ruler in Israel,
whose coming forth is from of old,
from ancient days. (Micah 5:2)

It was a typical Monday during my sophomore year in high school. I sat down at my normal lunch table with my tray of greasy mozzarella sticks and fruit snacks. One by one, all the usual friends dropped their trays down too.

My friend Sara immediately launched into a story that happened over the weekend. Scott jumped in too, then Brandon, and Lily, and a few others. I realized that they had all been together at the same event, and I had not been invited. I sat there, laughing when they did, acting like I had been there too—desperate to hide what my heart was really doing, beating faster and faster with anxiety.

Why hadn't I been invited? Why had they forgotten me? Why was I not good enough to be a part of the group? In a sea of green lunch trays, I felt the smallest I had ever felt. No one wanted me.

THE GOD WHO MAKES PROMISES

In Micah 5:2, the prophet speaks to the Israelites, descendants of the people Moses had led out of Egypt centuries before. Since then, they've had kings from the line of David to lead them through wars. David's son Solomon has built a magnificent temple where the people could worship God. However, the kingdom God had given them has been divided in two: Israel to the north and Judah to the south.

Through Micah, God warns the inhabitants of the south that they will lose their home as a response to their disobedience to him. Micah tells them that hard times are coming, but he also shares a unique prophecy that holds a unique promise.

Read the verse again and see if you can find it. Is there anything (more specifically, any *place*) that sounds familiar?

For the first time, we hear that God's promised Messiah, "ruler in Israel, whose coming forth is from old," will be born in Bethlehem.

This is big news! Micah's original audience would remember that their beloved King David was also from Bethlehem, a clan that everyone thought was "too little" to have anything good come from it. And yet David had been the greatest king of Israel. Now Micah is telling God's people that King David was only a small foretaste of the greater King to come.

THE GOD WHO KEEPS PROMISES

The life of Jesus is the tangible expression of this promise! Jesus, born in the small town of Bethlehem to very normal, earthly parents, lived a perfect life so that your imperfect one would not be held against you. He died a death that perfectly paid for your debt of disobedience to God. And his resurrection ensured that eternal life in his kingdom would be a gift for you, one who might often feel "not enough" or "too much" to be a part of the "in" crowd at school.

Micah's prophecy tells us that God can make something *great* come from something *not good enough*. Our God, ruler of the universe and creator of all things, makes promises to you and to me that are seemingly impossible. God tells us that he uses things and people that everyone else would consider "too little" or "not enough" or "too much" or "too imperfect" to bring to life his plan for his glory and your future.

Because of Jesus's saving work on your behalf, you are *not* too much or, like Bethlehem, "too little" to know and experience the Kingdom of God ruling in your life. May this Christmas season remind you of that truest of truths.

QUESTIONS FOR REFLECTION

1. When you think of being "too little," what imagery pops in your mind? Can you remember a time where you felt like you were not enough?
2. Jesus was born in humble circumstances to show us the lengths he would go to have a relationship with us. How would your perception of your life change if you started believing that God was doing *intentional* things with you and your life?
3. Is there someone in your life who might be able to show you the ways God is using your ordinary life in and for his kingdom? Write his or her name down and start seeking out ways to talk to them about it!

CLOSING PRAYER

Father, I give you praise for how you work in the world and in my life for your glory and for my good. Thank you for your Son, Jesus, whose willingness to be born in a humble town in humble circumstances has given me access to a full relationship and eternity with you. Would you remind me that I am not "too little" or "too anything" for you?

Day 10

Longing to Believe

Ben Birdsong

"Therefore, the Lord himself will give you a sign.
Behold, the virgin shall conceive and bear a son,
and shall call his name Immanuel." (Isaiah 7:14)

Have you ever wondered whether or not God is real?

Maybe you've never felt comfortable enough to let this question slip from your lips. Sometimes we can feel alone in our doubt, as though our questions make us less faithful Christians. Or maybe the overwhelming nature of your circumstances is blocking your view of God, your sense of his nearness and love.

THE GOD WHO MAKES PROMISES

When God spoke his promise through Isaiah in the verse above, one of Israel's worst kings, Ahaz, was facing his enemies in battle. Ahaz had rebelled against God by worshipping idols and engaging in the pagan practices of the surrounding nations. In a moment of desperation in battle, Ahaz likely wanted to know whether God was with him.

Although Ahaz had repeatedly turned away from God, the Lord graciously gives him a sign: a virgin will have a son who will be called Immanuel, or "God with us." God intends this promise to encourage Ahaz and all of Judah that God truly is with them, not only in their current moment of need, but forever. Sadly, Ahaz refuses to put his trust in God. He continues to worship the gods of the nations instead, even asking a pagan king for rescue (2 Chronicles 28:16). Yet even in the face of Ahaz's unfaithfulness, God promises to be faithful to his people.

THE GOD WHO KEEPS PROMISES

Fast-forward several hundred years. At the beginning of Matthew's Gospel, we read how God fulfills the Immanuel sign through an engaged couple named Joseph and Mary. An angel announces to Mary that she will have a baby who is from God. It must have felt impossible for Mary and Joseph to wrap their heads around this once-in-an-eternity miracle. Matthew tells us that Joseph had planned to divorce Mary quietly in order not to make a scene. But the Lord comes to him to confirm Mary's story (Matthew 1:19–20).

God is present with Mary and Joseph, even as they struggle to understand what he is doing. He reminds them of his presence as they welcome the fulfillment of Isaiah 7 in the person of Jesus, Immanuel, or "God with us" (Matthew 1:23).

The message of Christmas is that Jesus came to be the *with us* God. After living a perfect life, Jesus died on the cross to remove the barrier of sin that separated us from God the Father. He rose again from the dead, defeating our sin and opening the door for Jesus to be with us forever in eternity.

The invitation of Immanuel is to know and believe you have a God who is with you in Jesus. When you find yourself in circumstances that seem too deep to bear or stuck in your own sin, Jesus is with you. When you feel confused about where God is in your pain, Jesus is with you. Though you may find yourself questioning God and wondering if his Word can be trusted, he is with you.

Jesus gave his life to be with us forever. We can trust him because he "will never leave nor forsake us" (Hebrews 13:5), no matter how many times we may silently question his presence.

QUESTIONS FOR REFLECTION

1. What circumstances in your life cause you to wrestle with doubt or even to question God's existence?
2. Do you know someone going through a difficult time that you can remind of the invitation of Immanuel?
3. How can you remind yourself today that Jesus truly is with you?

CLOSING PRAYER

Lord, sometimes it is hard for me to believe that you are with me, or even that you are real. Thank you for sending Jesus to demonstrate your presence and care. Please give me eyes to see your presence with me in all moments of life. Help me to trust and rely on you today. Amen.

Day 11

Longing for Light

Liz Edrington

The people who walked in darkness
have seen a great light;
those who dwelt in a land of deep darkness,
on them has light shone. (Isaiah 9:2)

When was the last time you looked for something in the dark? Maybe you were playing flashlight tag or making your way to the bathroom in the middle of the night. It's disorienting to rely on senses other than our sight. We listen for footsteps. Our fingertips slide across walls and door frames. Our depth perception is off. The darkness can feel invasive, like it's pressing in.

THE GOD WHO MAKES PROMISES

In Isaiah 9, we read about "people who walked in darkness." These were people who weren't worshipping or following the one true God, Yahweh. They were looking to other things for hope. They asked other gods to provide what they needed. They relied on leaders of nearby nations to help them fight off their enemies.

Our modern culture tells us to look to *ourselves* when we have a need. We're supposed to persevere through hard seasons of exams, difficult family dynamics, breakups, and college applications, all from our own strength. We're told that freedom means total independence to choose our own destiny.

We're told to create our own hope and rely on our inner light as the kings of our own little worlds.

Well, I'm not sure how that's working out for you, but it sure hasn't worked well for me. I find that my world gets darker the more I try to manage my own future and muster up my own hope. Anxiety rises. And the more I try on my own to untangle it, the bigger the knot grows. I need rescue from the outside. I need a greater King to break in with order and light.

Thankfully, this is exactly what God is promising to do in Isaiah.

THE GOD WHO KEEPS PROMISES

The Bible is the true story of this promise unfolding. John 1 describes King Jesus, God with skin on, coming into the world *as light*. Revelation 22:5 says that in eternity, God himself will *be the light* by which we see everything else. Jesus enters into the dark, unmanageable, impossible places in us and in creation. He changes everything.

During Advent, we're invited to pay attention to our *waiting* for Christ's birth and for the day when he will return. We can tell God everything we're waiting for—places where we long for healing, change, peace, and connection. This might look like telling him about our desire for our anxiety to go away. Our hope that our parents will stop fighting. Our dreams of getting into a particular college.

For me, it can be hard to acknowledge these places of longing and waiting and entrust them to God. It's like walking through a dark, scary tunnel. But the Light of Life walks with me. Like little pools of light that spill into the tunnel, experiences of God's goodness catch the corner of my eye and interrupt the inky blackness. A friend checks in on me. A beautiful sunset grabs my attention. My dog snuggles up to me just because. I am reminded that darkness will not be the end of the story because Light has *already* broken through.

Instead of looking to ourselves for the light this Christmas, may we bring these places of lonely darkness to Jesus. The Light of the World became intimately familiar with these experiences. He knows how heavy the dark can feel. And he gives us the hope that we *will* see ultimate healing and fulfillment one day when we are face-to-face with him. Then, the darkness will be swallowed up forever as we celebrate eternally (Revelation 22:5).

QUESTIONS FOR REFLECTION

1. Think of a time when you can remember light flooding into a dark place. What was it like?
2. What is appealing about being our own kings? Yet what are some of the difficulties of trying to control our destiny?
3. Our God rules as King over even the darkness in our lives. Where in your life do you long for Jesus to shine his light right now?

CLOSING PRAYER

Jesus, would you cause us to walk in your light? Would you help us to trust you as the eyes of our hearts struggle to adjust to reality with you as King? Give us your hope and peace, we pray, and please break into the dark, seemingly impossible places in our lives. Show us the beauty we have in you, Light of the World. Amen.

Day 12

Longing to Lighten the Load

Chelsea Kingston Erickson

For to us a child is born,
to us a son is given;
and the government shall be upon his shoulder,
and his name shall be called
Wonderful Counselor, Mighty God,
Everlasting Father, Prince of Peace.
Of the increase of his government and of peace
there will be no end,
on the throne of David and over his kingdom,
to establish it and to uphold it
with justice and with righteousness
from that time forth and forevermore.
The zeal of the LORD of hosts will do this. (Isaiah 9:6–7)

I still remember the day in my junior English class when I saw an image of the Greek god Atlas holding the world on his shoulders. I identified with the mythological Atlas. Pressure to measure up socially, academically, and even as a Christian was like a physical weight I carried on my shoulders.

I'm sure you can relate. The demands of schoolwork and the burden to excel in sports or the arts can weigh you down. It's hard to live up to the expectations of our friends, parents, coaches, teachers, and youth workers.

In addition to all this performance pressure, we now carry the Internet in our pockets. As a teenager, I didn't have the kind of exposure you do to matters of social justice, environmental concerns, wars, politics, and more. When our feeds constantly remind us that things are not as they should be, we can become discouraged or anxious. It can feel as though it's all up to us to solve the world's problems.

Does it ever feel like the weight of the world is on your shoulders?

THE GOD WHO MAKES PROMISES

At the time Isaiah was writing, God's people were feeling the weight of their circumstances and their sin. Israel had shamefully neglected to keep God's laws, worshipping idols instead. Their land was filled with injustice, such as exploiting the vulnerable (Isaiah 1:17) and neglecting the poor (Isaiah 3:13–15). Their political leaders—kings like Ahaz—had failed them for generations, leading them deeper into idolatry and injustice. In Isaiah chapters 7 and 8, God tells his people to prepare for the darkness of exile: foreign nations will carry them off on account of their unfaithfulness.

Into this heaviness, the prophet Isaiah announced good news of a coming Savior (Isaiah 9:6).

The word *government* comes from the Hebrew word for dominion, reign, or struggle. It's a royal term that speaks to the rule of a king. Isaiah proclaimed that a good and faithful King would bear Israel's struggle. He would take the weight of the whole world on his strong shoulders so the Israelites wouldn't have to carry it themselves.

The promised King's reign would be one of peace and not of war. His government would be an everlasting one marked by justice (all things being made right) and righteousness (all people doing right).

THE GOD WHO KEEPS PROMISES

This King has indeed come into our world to reign on David's throne—Jesus, our *Wonderful Counselor, Mighty God,*

Everlasting Father, Prince of Peace. At Christmas, we remember how Jesus came as a baby to experience life in this broken world as we do. But Christmas also points us forward to the second coming of Jesus, when he will finally return to make all things right!

In our fallen sinfulness, we believe we can somehow prove ourselves by how we perform. Likewise, we sometimes imagine that we have the strength and power within ourselves to right the world's wrongs. The reality is that we need a Rescuer, and we have one in Jesus. Because of Jesus, we can rest. We don't have to carry the weight of the world—or of our lives—alone.

When you feel the pressures of life and the concerns of the world pressing in on you, remember that our God has come in the person of Jesus to carry your burdens. Jesus has rescued you through his life, death, and resurrection in your place. There is a day coming when the world itself will be remade, and then our Prince of Peace will fully establish the kingdom Isaiah promised so long ago. John depicts it this way:

> Then the seventh angel blew his trumpet, and there were loud voices in heaven, saying, "The kingdom of the world has become the kingdom of our Lord and of his Christ, and he shall reign forever and ever." (Revelation 11:15)

QUESTIONS FOR REFLECTION

1. What pressures or concerns in your life feel like a heavy weight to carry around?
2. How could you hand these things over to Jesus, your Burden-Bearer (Isaiah 9: 6 and 53:4)?
3. According to Isaiah 9, how is Jesus's kingdom different from the political kingdoms in our world today?

CLOSING PRAYER

King Jesus, our Prince of Peace, thank you for taking the weight of the world upon your shoulders, and my sin and shame as well. Forgive me for trying to prove myself or for trying to solve the world's problems on my own. Help me to trust in you until you return.

Day 13

Longing for Flourishing

Liz Edrington

There shall come forth a shoot from the stump of Jesse,
and a branch from his roots shall bear fruit.
And the Spirit of the LORD shall rest upon him,
the Spirit of wisdom and understanding,
the Spirit of counsel and might,
the Spirit of knowledge and the fear of the LORD.
And his delight shall be in the fear of the LORD. (Isaiah 11:1–3a)

I once went on a beautiful hike that started from the rim of a mountain. The first part of the walk involved careful steps down a rocky, root-filled slope. I could see a blanket of broccoli-like treetops beneath me. Then, after a couple of minutes, branches began to swipe at my face as I descended farther and farther.

After a while, I could no longer see where the twisting path ahead was leading. I'd turn a corner and all of a sudden, giant house-high boulders would appear, looming over me. They were fascinating, evoking my curiosity and my desire to climb.

As I looked up, I saw a sapling growing from the side of the boulder. Life had sprung forth from a rock. The impossible had happened.

I thought of the impossible places in my life. Imagining healing in my relationship with a particular family member felt impossible. I was stuck in a season of depression that made hope feel impossible too. For you, it might be persistent anxiety. Or it could be a desire to have a best friend, or to belong.

My mind traveled to the passage in the book of Isaiah in which the prophet describes a shoot (a tiny plant) coming up from the stump of Jesse, King David's father.

THE GOD WHO MAKES PROMISES

Imagine a tree that has been axed down to a stump. It is dead. It isn't good for anything but grinding up for mulch. It's a bit of a hopeless sight.

Yet *this* is the metaphor Scripture uses to describe the origin story of Jesus, the One True King.

God had promised his people that a descendant from David's family would rule forever (2 Samuel 7:16). And the people *longed* for the flourishing and freedom that came with living under a good king. Their already tiny kingdom had been divided in two. They'd faced enslavement, famine, and war. The future looked bleak.

Yet God's promise rang in their hearts: a Messiah was coming to bring an end to all evil and make peace with the whole world (Isaiah 11:1–11). In a seemingly impossible place— the nearly dead family line of King David—God promised to bring life.

THE GOD WHO KEEPS PROMISES

The genealogy we read at the beginning of the book of Matthew tells the story. In the person of Jesus, the Son of God born to Mary in Bethlehem, a shoot sprouts up from the dead family tree of David—just like the tree growing out of my craggy boulder. God brings life to seemingly impossible places.

As the Messiah (the promised rescuer of God's people), Jesus will continue this pattern of bringing life from dead, broken places. In his crucifixion and resurrection, he forever ends the curse of death by conquering it altogether. His empty tomb becomes a sapling-growing stump that brings the hope of eternal life for all who believe in him.

It is a beautiful thing that our God uses death to bring life. The ugly, painful, sometimes unbearable stumps in our lives are never without hope because our living Lord, the Messiah of Israel, is reigning on his throne.

This means our broken friendships are not without hope. Our embarrassing failures are not without hope. Our lack of popularity, or athletic skill, or desired body type—none of these is without hope. In fact, *these* are the very places our God is at work. Growing us. Healing our hearts to make them more able to give and receive love. No injustice goes unseen. No evil will prevail. *Peace is guaranteed*, thanks to our Good King who is coming to reign forever.

QUESTIONS FOR REFLECTION

1. Where else in Scripture do we see God bringing something from nothing? (Consider Genesis 17:15–19 and 21:1–2, Exodus 16:1–4, Matthew 14:15–21, and John 9:1–6.)

2. Can you think of someone else's stump story—in which God brought healing, change, or something beautiful from a seemingly impossible situation?

3. What is something in your life that seems like a dead stump? Take time to talk with God about this situation, asking him to bring life from death.

CLOSING PRAYER

King Jesus, you are the one who wastes nothing. You are able to bring life from death, sight from blindness, and beauty from pain. We pray that you would meet us in the dead stumps in our lives, and that you would help us to offer them to you for your kingdom's sake. Please use the seemingly impossible places in our lives to make your love, peace, and glory even more present in this world. We pray in Jesus's name. Amen.

Day 14

Longing for a Hero

Joey Turner

Behold my servant, whom I uphold,
my chosen, in whom my soul delights;
I have put my Spirit upon him;
he will bring forth justice to the nations.

He will not cry aloud or lift up his voice,
or make it heard in the street;

a bruised reed he will not break,
and a faintly burning wick he will not quench;
he will faithfully bring forth justice.

He will not grow faint or be discouraged
till he has established justice in the earth;
and the coastlands wait for his law. (Isaiah 42:1–4)

Anxiety to the point of fainting. Discouragement that does not lift. Abuse that leaves you bruised. Faithlessness like a candle about to go out. Whether it is the constant comparison of yourself to others, your looks to their looks, your accomplishments to their accomplishments, or your inability to break a cycle of sin that you hate, you can't take it anymore. You sense that your candle is about to go out. You feel like a reed about to break. Your embers are barely burning.

THE GOD WHO MAKES PROMISES

At the time of Isaiah's writing, God's people are worshipping idols they have made with their own hands (Isaiah 2:8, 42:7). They have become enslaved to these false gods. In their captivity they are weak. They need someone who will deliver them and destroy their enemy. They need someone who is able to take down a giant without destroying the prisoners underfoot.

Who can deliver such a victory? The One who created the heavens and the earth, and he who gives breath to all people (42:5). How is God going to deliver his people? Through his beloved chosen servant, who is in himself a new covenant with God's people (42:6). He will open the eyes of those who are blinded and bring out the prisoners who sit in the darkest dungeon (42:7).

To a struggling Israel, Isaiah speaks of a future event. He speaks of God's chosen servant (42:1) who "will not grow faint or be discouraged till he has established justice in the earth" and in so doing set prisoners free (42:4).

THE GOD WHO KEEPS PROMISES

Enter Jesus. Our hero. Our rescuer. The one who specializes in creating bonfires out of what looks like ashes. The one who renews the strength of the weak. The one who heals the wounds of the bruised. The one who encourages us to keep persevering through difficult seasons.

Now, long after Isaiah was written, we look back and see that Jesus is the beloved servant God promised. The path he took for our salvation to kill our great Enemy, and to free us from bondage to our idols, was one of suffering. In order to defeat Satan, the beloved servant of God was broken, and his flame was extinguished. Yet he did not remain broken and quenched. Defeating the great Enemy, Christ resurrected with a body that will never break again and a flame that cannot be extinguished.

God sent a redeemer for our dilemma, not a to-do list. God sent a reconciler, not a mantra. God's means of transformation in your life comes by faith in the sufficiency of his Son, not in your own effort. Jesus suffered for you. Jesus endured for you. And, Jesus defeated the Enemy for you.

God promises you will not be overwhelmed by your discouragement or grow faint. Your pain is real, but it will not break you. Your light is faint, but it will not go out because your God who promises to take you by the hand and *keep you* will also keep his promise. Jesus himself will be the light within you that shines in your neighborhood, your home, and your school.

QUESTIONS FOR REFLECTION

1. What is the most discouraging thing in your life right now?
2. When you are discouraged, what do you do or where do you go to feel better?
3. How does God's promise of sending his Son restore hope and joy to your life?

CLOSING PRAYER

God, you upheld your Son Jesus Christ. Uphold me now. Father, Christ was your chosen one. Remind me that you have chosen me in him. Your soul delights in Jesus, and so it delights in me. Your Spirit dwells in me. Thank you for promising to take me by the hand and keep me. Thank you for being the light in a world full of darkness. Amen

Day 15

Longing for a Remedy

Katie Polski

But he was pierced for our transgressions;
he was crushed for our iniquities;
upon him was the chastisement that brought us peace,
and with his wounds we are healed. (Isaiah 53:5)

Have you ever downplayed your own wrongdoing?

Once when I was in high school, the answers to an upcoming test were being passed around in the hallway. When the sheet made its way to me, I quickly looked through the answers. I justified my actions because all my other friends had looked and because I had only *glanced*. When our teacher confronted us, one student defiantly asked, "Is it really that big of a deal?"

The temptation is to make light of our daily struggles, and perhaps even to believe the lie that we're not actually terrible sinners who are in need of rescue. Is our sin really "that big of a deal?"

Whether you have experienced a period of intense anger or jealousy, or whether you struggle daily to turn away from lust or dishonesty, we all battle spiritual sickness. Unlike physical illnesses, our battle against sin emerges from our own fallen nature. We often want to blame someone else for our sin, as if this will soothe our conscience. The humbling truth is that your sin is *your* sin, and it *is* a big deal.

THE GOD WHO MAKES PROMISES

God promised a remedy in the form of a Savior who would come to earth and pay the penalty for our sin, completely curing our spiritual sickness.

To understand how awesome Isaiah's words are, we have to briefly put ourselves in the shoes of the Israelites as they listened to Isaiah's prophecy. Isaiah's job was to remind God's people of the covenant that God had made with them. The covenant was kind of like a marriage—it was an agreement between God and his people. God promised that he would be their God, protecting them and always loving them, and God will never break his promise.

Israel's responsibility was faithfulness and obedience to God. But many broke this promise, turning away from God to serve idols. Isaiah reminded Israel of God's faithfulness, and he gave the Israelites warnings about what would happen if they continued to rebel. The severe warnings may have caused some to wonder whether there was any hope.

This is where God's amazing promise comes in. Isaiah tells God's people that one day a Messiah would come to pay the penalty for every wrongdoing, healing them fully and completely from their sin.

THE GOD WHO KEEPS PROMISES

God fulfilled his promise eight hundred years later when a baby was born in Bethlehem.

Through Jesus the promise came true that a Savior would come to die in order to bring peace and healing. Jesus was pierced *for you*. He was crushed and chastised *for you*. Jesus suffered in an agonizing way not for his sin, but for *yours.*

Why?

Because God loves you more than you can comprehend. If you have trusted in Jesus, he is not keeping track of your sins. No. Jesus has already completely and fully paid for the sins of those who belong to him—both past and present. God knows the worst things you've ever done or thought, and because of Jesus, he loves you unconditionally, *no matter what*.

Because of Christ's sacrifice, you have peace with God. You can shed the weariness caused by trying to make yourself worthy; God the Father calls you *his child* even on the worst days. You can throw away condemnation and shame for past sins; Jesus has paid for every one of them.

We need Jesus every day to resist sin; we cannot do it by our own strength. And we also desperately need the peace that comes through forgiveness.

Jesus provides this because he loves you. He took on flesh in order to die the death that we deserve. There has not been, nor will there ever be, a greater sacrifice than the one Jesus has made for *you*, beloved child of God.

QUESTIONS FOR REFLECTION

1. Is it hard or easy for you to believe that every last one of us is deeply afflicted by sin, equally in need of Jesus's salvation?

2. When you consider that Jesus's sacrifice fully and completely covers our transgressions and our iniquities, what response does this stir up in you? Read Ephesians 2:8–10.

3. If you feel peace with God this Christmas season, how does this peace make a difference in your day-to-day activities? If not, what do you think are some of the barriers to experiencing this peace?

CLOSING PRAYER

Jesus, open my eyes to the depth of my sin. Only when I have a right view of myself as a sinner do I understand my need for you. Thank you for coming to earth and for sacrificing yourself in order to set me free from the bondage of sin. I love you, Jesus.

Day 16

Longing to Overcome

Ben Sciacca

The Spirit of the LORD God is upon me,
because the LORD has anointed me
to bring good news to the poor;
he has sent me to bind up the brokenhearted,
to proclaim liberty to the captives,
and the opening of the prison to those who are bound;
to proclaim the year of the LORD's favor,
and the day of vengeance of our God;
to comfort all who mourn;
to grant to those who mourn in Zion—
to give them a beautiful headdress instead of ashes,
the oil of gladness instead of mourning,
the garment of praise instead of a faint spirit;
that they may be called oaks of righteousness,
the planting of the LORD, that he may be glorified. (Isaiah 61:1–3)

Depression is paralysis and darkness.

For almost three years, lying in my bed felt like resting in a coffin. I was awake and self-aware, but I felt powerless and teetering on the cusp of death as I lay my head on my pillow. With great effort I would rise, eat, work, and speak to others. But the simplest actions of life required white-knuckled grit and ragged cries to God for help.

Even if you've never personally struggled with depression, you can see that the world is broken and hurting. Every day people are struggling with mental health concerns, hopelessness, confusion, and a deep sense of loneliness. Others battle a tremendous sense of guilt, shame, or even abandonment. It's likely that in your own life you have ebbed and flowed with feelings of discouragement or even despair. We need hope from outside ourselves.

THE GOD WHO MAKES PROMISES

Isaiah 61 reminds us that the Lord is invested in the rescuing and deliverance business.

Isaiah's promises came during a time when the nation of Israel was under horrendous threat by the Assyrians. This neighboring menace was barbaric and brutal to those they conquered. Isaiah's words about a Comforter to come were sweet promises of light and hope to a people surrounded by evil, violence, and darkness.

Eventually the Assyrians defeated the ten northern tribes of Israel and hauled them into exile. At times, we too find ourselves horribly surrounded by dire circumstances. In such a season, we need someone who will overcome our troubles for us.

THE GOD WHO KEEPS PROMISES

In Jesus, we see how God fulfilled the promise of living and lasting hope in Isaiah 61. When he began his earthly ministry, Jesus announced that he was the one Isaiah had foretold. He was the one who would bring good news to the poor, bind up brokenhearted people, provide liberty to captives, and liberate those who were bound (Luke 4:16–21).

The baby born in Bethlehem was the Son of God. He became physically present with his people to deliver them from suffering and darkness. His crucifixion, burial, and resurrection established his victory over sin and Satan, once and for all. We are not alone in our suffering. Our God is not unfamiliar with our pain, nor is he indifferent. He cares greatly, and he knows experientially what it means to suffer.

Shortly before Jesus died on the cross, he made an astounding promise to his disciples and to us: "I have said these things to you, that in me you may have peace. In the world you will have tribulation. But take heart; I have overcome the world" (John 16:33).

Depression, loneliness, shame, guilt, fear, and frustration do not have the final say. Some of these battles we face may remain with us all our lives, but the good news of Jesus Christ is that his grace and power reign more powerful than the forces that hold us down. He is coming again to make all things right.

In this broken world, we don't always receive the permanent deliverance or restoration for which we cry out. But the Lord promises that a day is coming when Jesus will finally and fully overcome the world.

Questions for Reflection

1. You might not be financially poor or battling a specific form of physical oppression, but can you think of some ways that you might be poor or oppressed spiritually?

2. What are some different challenges you are facing in your life right now? How can Christ's promise that he has "overcome this world" give you hope in those situations?

3. Are there people in your life who are facing hard times? What are some ways that you can bring them the hope of Jesus during this Advent season?

Closing Prayer

Dear Lord, sometimes life is both hard and confusing. At times I feel weighed down by darkness.

Thank you for coming to earth to shine a bright light. Thank you for overcoming this world and all of its brokenness by allowing yourself to be broken on the cross. Please continue to shine your light in my life and in this world. Amen.

Day 17

Longing for Right Relationships

Mark Howard

"Behold, the days are coming, declares the LORD,
when I will raise up for David a righteous Branch, and he shall
reign as king and deal wisely, and shall execute justice
and righteousness in the land. In his days Judah will be saved,
and Israel will dwell securely. And this is the name by which
he will be called: 'The LORD is our righteousness.'"
(Jeremiah 23:5–6)

Few pains cut as deep as hurt within a close relationship. The holidays can make this pain even worse. I know from personal experience, and I expect you do too.

This is what sin does—it painfully ruins relationships. As soon as Adam and Eve sin in the Garden of Eden (Genesis 3:16–19), we find them arguing and hiding from one another and God (Genesis 3:7–13). In the very next story, Cain murders his brother Abel in jealousy (Genesis 4). Throughout the narrative of the Old Testament, we see how sin mires family relationships.

THE GOD WHO MAKES PROMISES

By the time of the prophet Jeremiah, things are bad for Israel. Their sin and broken relationships are catching up with them as the nation faces threats from without and within. And yet, alongside the woes and warnings, God gives Jeremiah a message of hope: God will provide a Savior.

Humankind has become like a branch that produces fruit leading to pain and injustice, but in Jeremiah's words, God promises a Branch that will bear fruit leading to life.

This Branch will be called, 'The Lord is our righteousness' (Jeremiah 23:6). The word *righteousness* often refers to moral goodness, or right-standing before God. But in an even deeper sense, the meaning of the Hebrew speaks to a rightness of relationships. Jeremiah is saying that alongside justice, the Messiah will restore our relationships, which have been frustrated by sin.

But for this to happen, sin and its ruinous effects have to be dealt with. The Messiah must willingly die for the sin of this world and be raised again to new life in order to bring about lasting justice and righteousness.

THE GOD WHO KEEPS PROMISES

This is what Jesus, the fulfillment of the Old Testament narrative, does for us in his death and resurrection. The Christmas birth narratives are designed to help us see Jesus as the true hope of God's people. He is a new son of Adam, an appointed member of Abraham's family, the promised king in the line of David. He's come to do what no other human could—to rescue God's people from our sin and to bring restored relationships with God and one another.

The apostle Paul puts it this way: because of the new life we have in Jesus, we have been given "the ministry of reconciliation" (2 Corinthians 5:18), we've been made "ambassadors for Christ" (v. 20), and we have become "the righteousness of God" (v. 21). All of these speak to our calling and our hope as followers of Jesus: to bring right-ness to our relationships with God, others, and this world.

The mind-blowing good news of the gospel is that while Jesus is the ultimate fulfillment of Jeremiah's hope, he invites us into his work of bringing wisdom, justice, and righteousness to the world.

So we don't lose hope. Yes, sin can still frustrate our relationships and bring deep pain—but Jesus has made a way for healing, redemption, and reconciliation. As those who trust in him, we are a part of his life-giving work.

One day, Jesus will return to make all things new. This new creation is depicted in Revelation 21 and 22 as a garden city in which there is a tree of life, the leaves of which are "for the healing of the nations" (Revelation 22:2). No longer will anything be marred by the curse of sin. Rather, Jesus's righteous rule will be complete as heaven and earth are united so that only blessing and abundance—and right relationships—remain.

QUESTIONS FOR REFLECTION

1. How can the hope of the new creation give us courage and strength to be ambassadors for Christ today?
2. Take a moment to reflect on where your sin has hurt a relationship. Is there something you can do today to bring healing, like praying for the Lord to change your heart, asking for forgiveness, or taking steps to right a wrong?
3. Where has someone else's sin brought you pain? Have you shared this hurt with God and a trusted, wise person? What can you do today to move toward forgiveness and keep your heart from growing bitter?

CLOSING PRAYER

Father God, thank you for relentlessly pursuing goodness and life for your people, despite our sin. Jesus Messiah, thank you for taking my sin with you into your grave and sharing your resurrection life with me. Holy Spirit, please give me your wisdom and strength so that I might be a faithful ambassador of reconciliation. Amen.

Day 18

Longing for a Good Shepherd

Cameron Cole

"For thus says the Lord GOD: Behold, I, I myself will search for my sheep and will seek them out. As a shepherd seeks out his flock when he is among his sheep that have been scattered, so I will seek out my sheep, and I will rescue them from all places where they have been scattered . . . I myself will be the shepherd of my sheep, and I myself will make them lie down, declares the Lord GOD." (Ezekiel 34:11–12, 15)

Remember when you were little and an adult made a promise that he or she didn't deliver on? Your teacher promised that today the class would go to the playground, and then she canceled. Perhaps your parents promised that you would get dessert that night or would go to a movie, but then they couldn't pull it off. You had eagerly anticipated it all day. Remember that frustration and disappointment?

Those well-meaning adults from our childhood disappointed us, but sometimes, as we grow older, we face a more sinister kind of broken promise. Our community and global leaders often say one thing and then do another, misleading us with empty promises.

THE GOD WHO MAKES PROMISES

Ezekiel addressed the divided nation of Israel as they faced disappointment in their leaders. The people had failed epically to keep God's covenant. They had worshipped idols and had rebelled against God's commands. Ezekiel says that God's people are like wayward sheep who need good leaders to help them pursue God and his ways.

But in Ezekiel 34, the prophet speaks of God's harsh judgment against Israel's promise-breaking leaders, calling them wicked shepherds. He accuses them of preying on their "sheep," slaughtering the vulnerable ones to satisfy their own appetites. In other words, the very people who were supposed to lead Israel in faithfulness to God have exploited and abused God's people instead.

But there is still hope for Israel. Although God will allow his people to go into exile, he himself will come to save his flock. In these verses from Ezekiel, God assures his people how their Savior will relate to them; he will be a diligent Shepherd, faithfully seeking those lost to sin and brokenness.

THE GOD WHO KEEPS PROMISES

This is exactly how Jesus behaved when he walked the earth. He gathered a motley band of disciples, including a tax collector, a political zealot, and a prostitute. He traveled tirelessly on foot all over Palestine, teaching and healing and making friends, all to reconcile us to himself.

Along the way, Jesus repeatedly told anyone who would listen that he was the Good Shepherd for whom they had been waiting for so long. As their Shepherd, he promised to go to extraordinary lengths to save them—even to the point of laying down his life for them (John 10:15). On the cross, the Good Shepherd became the Lamb of God, fulfilling all those promises, dying as the perfect sacrifice for their sins and ours.

Our God is a Father who will never be unable or unwilling to keep his promises to us. He is the only leader who fully keeps his promises. If facing death on a cross won't make him reconsider doing what he said he would do, then nothing will stop him from keeping his Word. "God is not man, that he should lie, or a son of man, that he should change his mind" (Numbers 23:19a).

Hear the voice of the Good Shepherd and follow him. He will never lead you astray.

QUESTIONS FOR REFLECTION

1. This passage shows us God's concern for those who live under harsh or abusive leaders. How does it help you to know God's heart to bring about justice for the vulnerable?

2. Are there promises God makes in Scripture that you find hard to believe? Why? Are there other promises God makes that you find easier to believe? Why is that?

3. In Matthew 18:12–14, Jesus tells the story of a shepherd who leaves ninety-nine sheep to go in search of one sheep that has been lost. What does this parable tell you about Jesus? What does it mean to you personally?

CLOSING PRAYER

Father, thank you for keeping every promise you've ever made in your perfect way and in your perfect time. Jesus, thank you for being both my Good Shepherd and the Lamb who takes away my sin. This Christmas, help me to keep both the manger and the cross in my heart so that I trust you more every day.

Day 19

Longing for Home

Ashley Kim

"I will make a covenant of peace with them. It shall be an everlasting covenant with them. And I will set them in their land and multiply them, and will set my sanctuary in their midst forevermore. My dwelling place shall be with them, and I will be their God, and they shall be my people. Then the nations will know that I am the LORD who sanctifies Israel, when my sanctuary is in their midst forevermore." (Ezekiel 37:26–28)

Have you ever felt homesick? Perhaps you missed home while at summer camp, on vacation, or on a mission trip. Maybe your family moved away from your hometown, or you're a student at a boarding school or studying abroad. Or perhaps you have simply been in a new, unfamiliar place and wished you could be back at home.

That longing for home, however sharp or soft, is no mistake. Home, after all, is where we find rest with loved ones in a familiar place. Home is where we feel comfortable, safe, and secure.

THE GOD WHO MAKES PROMISES

The people of Israel were well acquainted with the pain of homesickness. Ezekiel was writing to a people who had been forcibly exiled from their home in Judah and taken to Babylon. A foreign army had destroyed the city of Jerusalem and its temple. The Israelites were cut off from their homeland and from the temple, where they had worshipped and enjoyed the presence of God.

Yet the Babylonian invasion was more than a random tragedy—it was God's judgment on Israel for their stubborn worship of other gods. Although God had patiently sent many prophets to Israel, the people continued in their evil ways. The destruction of Israel was an expression of God's justice and holiness. He would not sit by and let Israel continue in their wickedness.

Into this mess of suffering and sin, grief and guilt, Ezekiel speaks the words of the Lord—words of immense, almost unbelievable hope.

Although Israel has been exiled, God promises to "set them in their land and multiply them" (Ezekiel 37:26), to bring them back home and prosper them. The Babylonian exile would not be the end of the story. God had a plan to restore the people of Israel again. Their homesickness would not be forever.

Israel's greatest problem was not being cut off from a physical home, but being cut off from God. While the physical distance between the people of Israel and their home could be measured, the spiritual distance between them and God could not be quantified. Israel deserved eternal separation from him. That's why God's promise to "set [his] sanctuary in their midst forevermore" (v. 26) is so striking.

How? How could a holy God dwell with an unholy people? Listen to how God describes himself: "I am the LORD who sanctifies Israel" (v. 28).

THE GOD WHO KEEPS PROMISES

To *sanctify* something is to make it holy. *God* is the one who makes Israel holy so he can dwell in their midst. The people's unholiness—and their separation from God—will be dealt with not by them, but by God. Instead of demanding that his people bridge the gap, God provides another way in Jesus Christ.

In Christ, God took on human flesh and dwelt in our midst. Jesus understood exile: he had nowhere to lay his head (Matthew 8:20), he was driven out from his own hometown (Luke 4:29), and he was rejected by his own people (Matthew 23:37–39). In his death, Jesus bore the wrath and rejection of God that the Israelites—and we—rightly deserved.

Anyone who believes in him will not only be cleansed of all sin, but in the words of Jesus, "my Father will love him, and we will come to him *and make our home with him*" (John 14:23). God is not distant; he dwelt on earth in the Person of Jesus and dwells now in our midst through his Spirit. When Jesus returns, we will live with him forever (Revelation 21).

In Christ, we find more than just forgiveness for our sins. We find full acceptance, love, and security—we find home.

QUESTIONS FOR FURTHER REFLECTION

1. What comes to mind when you think about home? How is this similar or different to how you view your relationship with Jesus?
2. Where do you tend to look for comfort, safety, and security? How does God offer a better home (see Psalm 84)?
3. In what ways do we already experience God's presence with us here and now? In what ways are we still waiting to experience the fullness of God's presence?

CLOSING PRAYER

Father, you are faithful to your promises. You did not abandon your people Israel, even in exile. Thank you for the compassion of Jesus Christ, who came to be with us. Thank you for the love of the Holy Spirit, who dwells within me. Help me to find comfort in your nearness today. Amen.

Longing for Victory

Seth Stewart

"I saw in the night visions,
and behold, with the clouds of heaven
there came one like a son of man,
and he came to the Ancient of Days
and was presented before him.
And to him was given dominion
and glory and a kingdom,
that all peoples, nations, and languages
should serve him;
his dominion is an everlasting dominion,
which shall not pass away,
and his kingdom one that shall not be destroyed."
(Daniel 7:13–14)

The book of Daniel was written by a man who didn't belong, living in a country that was not his home. Even if you're not a refugee like Daniel, I'm sure you've felt disgusted by politics, alienated from your family, out-of-place among your friends, or just plain alone. I'm sure there have been times when you've felt displaced by a culture that's hostile to your faith, even if it's not trying to harm your body. If you have, you're in a perfect position to slip into Daniel's shoes.

And if you have not yet, you likely will when you leave home for the first time or go to college. At some point, you too may feel as though you've been dropped into a culture you don't fully understand. You may experience working for someone who wants to indoctrinate you into a different vision of reality.

As you live in our modern world, you have a lot in common with Daniel.

THE GOD WHO MAKES PROMISES

God encourages Daniel with two dreams. The first is horrifying, but the second is hopeful. In the first, four mutant beasts battle each other for dominance. In the second, an all-powerful King delegates his power to a "son of man" who defeats the monsters.

Throughout Daniel, monsters often stand for evil empires. We might not have such close encounters with blatant evil the way Daniel did, but we experience forms of it all the time, even if indirectly. School shootings, violent wars fought overseas, and morally bankrupt governments seem like forces too strong to overcome and are all examples of the "monsters" Daniel saw in his visions. But the good news of the second vision is that they are nothing compared to the cloud-riding son of man, the Ancient of Days.

In the Old Testament, clouds are a symbol of God's presence and power. Clouds cover Mount Sinai. A pillar of clouds protect Israel from Egypt. God's presence fills the tabernacle as a cloud. David sings that God "makes the clouds his chariot" (Psalm 104:3). The cloud-rider is somehow both a son of man and God himself. When he takes his throne, the monsters are obliterated.

THE GOD WHO KEEPS PROMISES

That's what we're celebrating at Christmas! God himself is born as the son of a man named Joseph. God, far from riding clouds in the sky above your pain, uses his power to enter *into* your pain. And even as Jesus is being beaten by unjust judges, he announces his victory over all powers that would oppress God's people. "I am . . . the Son of Man seated at the right hand of Power, and coming with the clouds of heaven" (Mark 14:62).

All of us are subject to powers, governments, people, and cultures beyond our control. But Daniel's message to both people in his day and to you is *don't lose heart*! Don't let rigged systems, unfair graders, biased coaches, chronic depression, or evil rulers discourage you. God will defeat the powers! He will vanquish the monsters. And he will rule forever because the Son of Man is coming on the clouds.

Jesus is the hoped for monster-crusher. In the face of vindictive rumors, chaotic shootings, and oppressive anxiety, he announces his ultimate rule over them all. They will all be brought to justice when Jesus comes again.

This Christmas, rejoice and hope! Jesus has defeated the powers of our present darkness, and he rules and reigns forever!

Questions for Reflection

1. What does Daniel 7:1–14 tell us about the kind of salvation God wants to give his people?
2. If Daniel was writing his book to you, what would he say about the monsters you encounter? Try to put Daniel's message of Jesus's coming into your own words, for your own situation.
3. Read Ephesians 1:19–2:7. Who sits beside Jesus on his throne? What does that mean for "monsters" in your life right now?

Closing Prayer

Holy Spirit, open my eyes to see the God who sits in power above all earthly kingdoms. Help me to see Jesus, the Son who rules over and is bringing to justice all the evil powers that cause me to feel overwhelmed.

Day 21

Longing for Unity

Ben Birdsong

"'"For thus says the LORD of hosts: Yet once more, in a little while, I will shake the heavens and the earth and the sea and the dry land. And I will shake all nations, so that the treasures of all nations shall come in, and I will fill this house with glory, says the LORD of hosts. The silver is mine, and the gold is mine, declares the LORD of hosts. The latter glory of this house shall be greater than the former, says the LORD of hosts. And in this place I will give peace, declares the LORD of hosts."'"
(Haggai 2:6–9)

With the buzz of her cell phone alarm, Susan woke up to another dreaded day. The one thing on her schedule—school—was enough to make her want to throw her phone across the room, pull the covers over her head, and block out the world.

Due to Susan's dad's job, her family had moved more times than she could count, and each time making friends became more difficult. She dreaded going another day to her new school, where she would walk the halls unnoticed and completely alone.

We all want to be welcomed to join the group. Throughout the Bible, we read about God's heart to rescue all people through Jesus the Messiah, answering this desire we all experience to be accepted and known.

THE GOD WHO MAKES PROMISES

Haggai 2 points to God's heart to welcome the nations, a theme throughout the Old Testament. From God's blessing Abraham (Genesis 12:1–3) to be a "blessing to the nations," God's plan for rescue through Jesus was not merely for the Israelites, but for people from all nationalities and ethnicities. Hundreds of years after Abraham, God spoke through the prophet Haggai, promising to "shake the nations" so that they too could be brought to worship before the throne of God.

Haggai wrote to the Jewish people who had just returned to their land from exile in Babylon. At the time of the exile, the Babylonians had carried off not only the Israelites, but all the sacred vessels of the temple as well. As the exiles gathered to rebuild the temple in Jerusalem, God reassured his people that he would once again fill the temple with his glory. A day was coming when all nations would bring their treasure to worship Israel's God as King. God wanted to remind his people that he wasn't only the God of Israel—no, he intended to rescue people from all nations.

THE GOD WHO KEEPS PROMISES

Through the coming of Jesus, God fulfilled the promises he had made to his people in Haggai's prophecy. Jesus would prove God's heart for people by living a perfect life, dying on the cross for our sins, and rising from the dead. He made a way for Israel and the nations to have a relationship with God and be included in His family.

A few months after Jesus's birth (Matthew 2:1–11), wise men from the East came to Jerusalem seeking to worship him with gifts of gold, frankincense, and myrrh. These gifts pointed to the life and ministry of Jesus. Gold signified Jesus's kingship. Frankincense, a fragrance used in worship, pointed to the truth that Jesus is God. Myrrh was a burial spice foretelling Jesus's death and resurrection. Jesus the Messiah is the heavenly King who came to die for the sins of people from all nations and to rise from the dead in order to give them a restored relationship with God.

Haggai described a new temple, which is not a building but a restored world when Jesus returns. The temple's greatness will surpass all that has come before. People from all nations will gather to worship Jesus, the heavenly King (Revelation 7:9), as he reigns forever on his throne

As followers of Jesus, we have received his gracious welcome into the kingdom of God. Because of this, we should be the first people who extend the welcome of Jesus's gospel to people from all places. God's grace and the rescue accomplished through Jesus in the gospel are open to all.

Questions for Reflection

1. What does it mean for you as a follower of Jesus to be included in Jesus's family? How does Jesus's family give you a sense of belonging?
2. Who are people on the outside of your world that God may be calling you to reach out to in friendship?
3. What would it look like for you to engage someone who comes from a different culture than you in a conversation about faith?

Closing Prayer

Lord, thank you for forgiving me and bringing me into your family. Help me to have eyes to see the people you have put around me who are outside of my circle of friends. Help me to build a friendship with someone different and share with them about Jesus's gracious welcome. Amen.

Day 22

Longing for Approval

Mac Harris

Rejoice greatly, O daughter of Zion!
Shout aloud, O daughter of Jerusalem!
Behold, your king is coming to you;
righteous and having salvation is he,
humble and mounted on a donkey,
on a colt, the foal of a donkey.
I will cut off the chariot from Ephraim
and the war horse from Jerusalem;
and the battle bow shall be cut off,
and he shall speak peace to the nations;
his rule shall be from sea to sea,
and from the River to the ends of the earth.
(Zechariah 9:9–10)

Have you ever found yourself at the center of attention, loved by your peers, only to find their backs turned against you the very next day? One day you hit the walk-off home run and the next, you strike out to lose? You go from the GOAT to *a goat* in the blink of an eye.

My senior year of high school, some teammates congratulated me for winning the election for class vice president. But the very next day, I walked into the locker room and overheard them mocking all the speeches—including mine!

Deep down we all know that human approval never lasts, and yet we still yearn for others to find us funny, put together, and worthy.

Of all people, Jesus knows exactly what it feels like to be celebrated one moment and vilified the next.

THE GOD WHO MAKES PROMISES

Writing around five hundred years before Jesus's birth, the prophet Zechariah saw hopelessness and despair everywhere he looked. God's people had returned to Jerusalem after a generation in exile, but they were still impoverished, oppressed, and insignificant. On the surface, it looked like God was nowhere to be found.

So when Zechariah cries out and prophesies, "Rejoice greatly . . . Behold, your king is coming to you," the Israelites would have perked up. *Could this be true? Is a king coming to save us?* At the same time, something about this king sounded . . . different.

THE GOD WHO KEEPS PROMISES

Fast-forward a few hundred years, and we see how Jesus fulfills Zechariah's prophecy when he rides a donkey (the royal mark of peace) into Jerusalem on Palm Sunday. The people praise God, worshipping Jesus as a triumphant King (Matthew 21). Rather than riding a war horse and raising an army to overthrow Israel's enemies, King Jesus rides a lowly donkey. He is the righteous and saving King Israel *needed*, but not the warrior they wanted.

Not even a week after Jesus had been hailed King, an angry mob in the same city of Jerusalem demands his death (Matthew 27:15–23). On Palm Sunday, Jesus is adored, praised, and hailed as King, but by Friday of that same week, he is mocked, scorned, and executed.

While Jesus understands the fickle nature of human approval better than any of us, he also promises that he will never stop loving us. We can never fall from his care, and God promises to never leave nor forsake his people (Deuteronomy 31:6).

When we look for fleeting approval on earth rather than eternal acceptance in heaven, we reveal what matters most to us, making it is harder to believe in Jesus. When we crave praise from our parents, laughs from our classmates, and high fives from our teammates, we place our worth in the approval of others, even though it will often leave us crushed and empty.

But when we put our trust in Jesus and find our value in him, we can rest in confidence. He who rode into Jerusalem on a donkey—who days later died on a cross—has once and for all called us *worthy*. His love for us is unmovable, eternal. And this Christmas, we wait for Jesus to return, to fulfill his promise to establish his peace on earth forever (Zechariah 9:10). As St. Augustine said, "our hearts are restless till they find their rest in thee."

We are his, and he is for us.

QUESTIONS FOR REFLECTION

1. Where do you find yourself seeking approval from friends, family, teachers, or teammates? What happens to us when we seek approval from other people?
2. What makes Jesus's approval different from that of others? What makes his kingdom different from that of others?
3. In your best moments, how do you think God views you? What about in your worst moments? How does his approval shape how you can live the rest of your life?

CLOSING PRAYER

Father God, thank you for your Word and for your faithfulness to fulfill your promises. As I celebrate the birth of Christ and anticipate his second coming, help me to lay my desire for human approval at your feet. Lead me to rest in your unwavering affection for me. Amen.

Day 23

Longing for Value

Carolyn Lankford

> Then I said to them, "If it seems good to you, give me my
> wages; but if not, keep them." And they weighed out as
> my wages thirty pieces of silver. Then the LORD said to me,
> "Throw it to the potter" . . . So I took the thirty pieces of silver
> and threw them into the house of the LORD, to the potter.
> (Zechariah 11:12–14a)

Have you ever been betrayed or sold out by a friend? I sure have. It is the worst kind of hurt.

During my junior year in high school, I ran for student council vice president. I lost the election because a close senior friend of mine decided to demonstrate his large heart at my expense. Two days before the election, my friend made a big show of throwing his support to my opponent, "the underdog," who won instead of me.

Jesus understands our suffering when friends betray us. He was sold out for thirty pieces of silver by a trusted friend, which led to his humiliating and painful death on a cross.

THE GOD WHO MAKES PROMISES

God promised this betrayal would happen hundreds of years before Jesus was born in Bethlehem. Zechariah spoke to the people of Israel as they were returning from exile to rebuild the city of Jerusalem and its temple.

In the prophetic books, God often tells his prophets to act out object lessons for his people. In chapter 11, we read how the Lord commanded Zechariah to become a shepherd to a flock of sheep, even though the sheep have already been doomed to the slaughterhouse. Zechariah obeys but becomes so disgusted by the cruelty of the other shepherds that he quits and asks for his wages. He receives thirty pieces of silver. That particular amount, the same amount that would be paid for a slave, is meant as a huge insult to Zechariah.

In asking Zechariah to act out this prophecy, God is saying that his shepherd would be rejected too. This promised shepherd, contrary to the other cruel shepherds, would lay down his life for the sheep.

THE GOD WHO KEEPS PROMISES

Fast-forward more than five hundred years, and Matthew tells us that the chief priests pay Judas thirty pieces of silver to betray Jesus (Matthew 26:14–16). Judas betrays Jesus with a kiss in the Garden of Gethsemane, leading to Jesus's death in the next hours. Realizing what he has set in motion, Judas feels remorse and throws the thirty coins back to the bribers in the Temple. The chief priests do not want the "blood money," so they use it to purchase a burial ground for outcasts called "Potter's field" (Matthew 27:3–8).

Thirty pieces of silver—the cost of a slave, blood money, the cost of a burial ground for outcasts—secured Jesus's crucifixion.

When we experience painful betrayals in our own lives, we can feel utterly devalued, as though we are on the clearance rack marked "everything must go." What's more, because of our sinful condition, we are like Zechariah's flock of sheep, unable to save ourselves.

But, by the grace of God, we are not marked down and put on the outcast rack. When we really screw up, or when we feel betrayed and worthless, the gospel assures us that God values us so much that he gave his Son in our place. Jesus was the one betrayed and cast aside so that by him, we never will be. This means we don't even have a price tag! To God we are priceless. And instead of death, he gives us life everlasting.

When you are "sold out" by the world, by bad shepherds in your life, what remains unchanged is the "not for sale" status you have in Jesus Christ.

At this moment in the Advent season, we are expecting this very truth: God, in his Son Jesus, is coming to be with us. We cannot shake him. He will never sell us to another shepherd or swap us out for a better deal. He has paid the price so we might be priceless.

QUESTIONS FOR REFLECTION

1. Have you felt betrayed? Have you been a betrayer? What does Jesus have to say to you on either account? What has he paid for you?

2. In what ways do you measure yourself? Measure others? Because of what Christ has done for you, you are priceless to God. How does that truth cause you to measure yourself and others differently?

3. The Bible is so beautiful and layered. Thirty pieces of silver is a recurring theme in the Bible from Exodus to Matthew. How might that inspire you to grow in God's Word?

CLOSING PRAYER

Dear Lord and my only Shepherd: Thank you for making yourself worth thirty silver coins so that I could be counted priceless through you. Forgive my wrong accounting of myself and of others. Please, Lord, let me live as one of your beloved sheep, paid for by your life, death, and resurrection in my place. Amen.

Day 24

Longing for Justice

Kevin Yi

"For behold, the day is coming, burning like an oven, when all the arrogant and all evildoers will be stubble. The day that is coming shall set them ablaze, says the LORD of hosts, so that it will leave them neither root nor branch. But for you who fear my name, the sun of righteousness shall rise with healing in its wings. You shall go out leaping like calves from the stall."
(Malachi 4:1–2)

As I write, there are at least two major international wars raging, and the tragedy and heartache of families caught in the cross fire is heartbreaking. The world seems to be groaning in pain. There is lament in our homeland, too, as we read about violent crime happening every day in our cities and states.

The present brokenness of our world makes me more aware than ever that the Christmas phrase "Peace on earth and goodwill to men" can sometimes feel like an impossible sentiment. And yet, when I hear it this season, it awakens a longing that is so palpable and real in my heart.

Maybe the unrest of the world isn't what causes you apprehension. Perhaps this longing for peace is more acute and more personal. Sometimes the pain we feel from living in the world can feel so overwhelming. Maybe you do what I do: it's just easier to live life on my phone, scrolling from meme to meme, searching for comfort in little pieces of humor.

This is why we need the promises found in Malachi 4.

THE GOD WHO MAKES PROMISES

The prophet Malachi speaks the last words recorded for God's people in the Old Testament. Then there would be a period of four hundred "silent" years in which the Lord would not speak through his prophets until the coming of Jesus.

Malachi's message is this: in times of deep trouble and despair, remember that the Lord is coming to rid the world of evil, and he is coming to be our ultimate hope (v. 1).

In the midst of suffering, it seems hard to believe that God cares about us, but he does. And though God's language at first glance might sound combative, think about who and what is on the receiving end of God's judgment: *the wicked, the arrogant, evildoers.* Everyone who has ever perpetrated a gross crime against another person will be duly punished and judged for their sins. To the persecuted Israelites, this is a profound affirmation. Justice will be paid in full. No one will get away with mistreating the vulnerable. God is just, and he promises this in no uncertain terms.

But then the prophecy pivots to someone, a "sun of righteousness" rising with "healing in its wings" (v. 2).

THE GOD WHO KEEPS PROMISES

Believe it or not, this strange-sounding promise is about Jesus, who came to heal and restore the world.

The Hebrew word that's translated as "wings" can also be translated as the "hem" or "edge" of a garment, which calls to mind a story about Jesus from Luke's Gospel. One day a woman who had been bleeding for twelve years comes to Jesus in the midst of a crowd and touches the edge of his cloak. Immediately, Jesus feels the power of healing go out from him, and he refuses to go on until the person who had touched him reveals herself. When the woman comes forward, Jesus tells her in his tender way, "Take heart, daughter, your faith has healed you."

Do you see it? Jesus is the "sun of righteousness," the perfect, obedient, radiant Son of God, with power to heal. And the same Jesus who lived, died, and resurrected on our behalf is coming again, radiant and beaming like the sun.

Malachi is telling us that when God rids the world of evil, violence, pain, and suffering, we will all be healed, and we will be filled with a joy unimaginable. When Jesus returns, everything that is good, true, and beautiful will be forever restored. And we'll leap with joy like the young calves in Malachi's prophecy.

The peace Jesus extends to us now is real, and we will experience it fully in the life to come. So let's wait in eager anticipation, hearts full of faith, for the sun of righteousness with healing in his wings.

QUESTIONS FOR REFLECTION

1. What events in our world today make you long for the God of justice to punish the wicked?
2. Does it surprise you that God's promises include both justice and healing? How do those two themes fit together in Malachi and elsewhere in the Old Testament promises?
3. Are there places in your own life in which you sense your need for God's healing? How can we reach out to touch the edge of Jesus's garment in prayer today?

CLOSING PRAYER

Father, it's your peace that we so desperately need in times like this. Open our hearts through faith to receive your assurance that you will make everything right one day. Heal our broken hearts, in Jesus's name we pray.

Day 25

Longing for Joy

Anna Meade Harris

And in the same region there were shepherds out in the field,
keeping watch over their flock by night. And an angel of the
Lord appeared to them, and the glory of the Lord shone around
them, and they were filled with great fear. And the angel said
to them, "Fear not, for behold, I bring you good news of great
joy that will be for all the people. For unto you is born this day
in the city of David a Savior, who is Christ the Lord. And this
will be a sign for you: you will find a baby wrapped in swaddling
cloths and lying in a manger." And suddenly there was with the
angel a multitude of the heavenly host praising God and saying,
"Glory to God in the highest, and on earth peace among those
with whom he is pleased!" (Luke 2:8–14)

Maybe you are reading this in the quiet of Christmas morning, before you join your family by the crackling fireplace.
You're excited for homemade cinnamon rolls or daydream-
ing about the contents of the brightly trimmed package with
your name on it.

Or maybe you're afraid that you'll open your bedroom
door to a day of disappointment. You anticipate that unmet
expectations and dashed hopes will be the gifts that keep on
giving, even on Christmas.

Either way, the angel's words to the shepherds are "good
news of great joy" . . . *for you.*

THE GOD WHO KEEPS PROMISES

In the course of one night, God turned the page of history to begin the redemption of the world that he first promised to Adam and Eve (Genesis 3:15). In his grace and mercy, God sent a Savior to be born in David's city, Bethlehem. He loved you and me so much that he sent his only Son to live the perfect life we could never live, die the death we deserve, and rise again to guarantee eternal life, keeping his promise to those who trust in him.

On that first Christmas morning in a manger, all of God's promises to us found their "yes!" in Jesus (2 Corinthians 1:20). Still, we have not yet seen every promise completely fulfilled. This is why Christians say we are living in the "now and not yet." For us, the "now" means living *after* the life, death, and resurrection of Jesus, but *before* he returns to transform the kingdom of this world into the everlasting kingdom of our Lord and Christ (Revelation 11:15).

"Now" we live in the tension of knowing that some of God's promises have been perfectly realized, and "yet" we're waiting to experience the completed redemption and restoration God has planned for us. That's why we still find ourselves longing for the bitter in our lives to be forever separated from the sweet. It's also why we can trust that it will be.

THE GOD WHO MAKES PROMISES

God closes his Word to us in the book of Revelation with more astounding promises—promises that are being fulfilled now, in our lifetime, and will be perfectly and completely fulfilled when Jesus returns:

God will dwell with human beings (Revelation 21:3).

He will wipe away every tear from our eyes (v. 4).

There will be no more death, or mourning, or crying, or pain (v. 4).

God is making all things new (v. 5).

In the fulfillment of every word he has ever spoken to us, to the satisfaction of every longing you've ever felt, Jesus will return: "Behold, I am coming soon." . . . "Surely, I am coming soon" (Revelation 22:7, 20).

Like our Lord and Savior Jesus Christ, these promises are trustworthy and true (21:5).

QUESTIONS FOR REFLECTION

1. Scripture encourages us to "remember the deeds of the LORD" (Psalm 77:11–12). Keep a record of God's promise-keeping in Scripture; ask God to help you see his steadfast love for you.
2. What have you learned about the character of God the Father that will help you live with faith and confidence in the "now and not yet"?
3. How does really *knowing* God's faithfulness affect how you think and feel about him?

CLOSING PRAYER

Father, I pray that the birth of Jesus we celebrate today will give me hope living in the "now and not yet." I believe that you keep your promises perfectly; help my unbelief (Mark 9:24). Your steadfast love and faithfulness, clearly seen in my Savior Jesus, fill me with great joy! Amen. Come, Lord Jesus!

rooted | ministry

Equipping and empowering churches and parents to faithfully disciple students toward lifelong faith in Jesus Christ.

www.rootedministry.com

Check out our: Articles, Books, Podcasts, Conference, YouTube, Curriculum, Training, Courses, and Mentorship Program